Hamster Holmes

On the Right Track

By **Albin Sadar**
Illustrated by **Valerio Fabbretti**

Ready-to-Read

Simon Spotlight
New York   London   Toronto   Sydney   New Delhi

For Ant—A. S.

To my grandparents—V. F.

SIMON SPOTLIGHT
An imprint of Simon & Schuster Children's Publishing Division
1230 Avenue of the Americas, New York, New York 10020
This Simon Spotlight edition February 2016
Text copyright © 2016 by Albin Sadar
Illustrations copyright © 2016 by Valerio Fabbretti
All rights reserved, including the right of reproduction in whole or in part in any form.
SIMON SPOTLIGHT, READY-TO-READ, and colophon are registered trademarks of
Simon & Schuster, Inc. For information about special discounts for bulk purchases, please contact
Simon & Schuster Special Sales at 1-866-506-1949 or business@simonandschuster.com.
Manufactured in the United States of America 0416 LAK
10 9 8 7 6 5 4 3 2
This book has been cataloged with the Library of Congress.
ISBN 978-1-4814-2043-3 (hc)
ISBN 978-1-4814-2042-6 (pbk)
ISBN 978-1-4814-2044-0 (eBook)

Hamster Holmes held up
two pencils.
"What do you think, Dr. Watt?
Which pencil is longer?"
he asked his firefly friend.
"Remember that things are not
always what they seem."
Dr. Watt scratched his head.

Dr. Watt used Morse code to get
his point across.
He blinked his light on and off
to form the dashes and dots.
A long flash of light was a dash.
A short flash of light was a dot.

"Dot-dot-dot-dot, dash-dash, dash-dash," flashed Dr. Watt. He pointed at a pencil.

"Actually," Hamster Holmes said, "the pencils are the *same* length! Holding them in a T-shape just makes one *seem* longer!"

That is when Springy Beaver,
a famous inventor, dropped by.
His hat flew off his head and
landed on the coatrack!
"You invented a hat that
hangs *itself* up?"
Hamster Holmes asked.

Springy nodded and said,
"But I'm here because my tools
and notebooks keep going missing.
I thought I was imagining it
because they always turn up again,
but yesterday I found paw prints!"

"I think someone is stealing my ideas," Springy went on.
"We're on the case!"
Hamster Holmes said.
"Let's go solve a mystery!"

They walked to Springy's home,
which was built over a spring.
They noticed prints on a window.
"Did you find prints in that room?"
Hamster Holmes asked.
"Yes, in my workshop!"
Springy said.

The workshop was full of inventions powered by springs. Springy pointed out the prints. They matched the prints outside. Hamster Holmes searched for clues while Dr. Watt did a detailed sketch.

Suddenly, there was a crash!
"That noise came from my garage,"
Springy said. "My secret invention
is hidden in there!"
They raced to the garage.

The suspect was gone but left
fresh prints in spilled paint.
Hamster Holmes asked Springy
if anything was missing.
"Nothing *springs* to mind!"
he replied. "How odd!"
Dr. Watt did a quick sketch
while Hamster Holmes followed
the trail.

"Where does that door lead?"
Hamster Holmes asked.
"To the indoor dock," Springy said.
"I built it so I can sail right into
my house!"

They ran to the dock, but the trail of prints ended by the water.
"If you can sail right *in*, a thief can sail right *out*!" said Hamster Holmes.
"If we hurry, maybe we can catch the suspect!"

"This is my fastest boat,"
Springy said. "Hop in!"
It didn't look very fast,
but when Springy began to pedal,
they sped off!

There were no other boats nearby.
"If the suspect had traveled by boat,
we would have caught up by now.
He or she must be a good swimmer!"
said Hamster Holmes.
Dr. Watt nodded.

"Or has a submarine!" Springy added, always thinking like an inventor.

"Indeed," began Hamster Holmes. "I'm sorry we lost the trail, Springy, but we'll keep working."

That night, the detectives looked in
a book about animal tracks.
They hoped to find an animal
whose tracks matched the prints
and who could swim.

Soon, Dr. Watt found tracks with
the same shape and number of toes
as the prints from the workshop.
"Ferrets do make tracks like these,"
said Hamster Holmes,
"but they are not strong swimmers."

Next they looked at the sketch of
the prints in the garage.
They looked different from the
ferret tracks.
"These look like weasel tracks!
Weasels like to swim, so we have
two suspects!" said Hamster Holmes.

"A ferret *and* a weasel were here?"
Springy asked the next day.
Hamster Holmes explained that
they wanted to take a closer look
since the weasel sketch was rushed.
Dr. Watt did a detailed sketch,
and they went on their way.

The detectives needed to think,
so they went to the wheel.
While Hamster Holmes ran,
Dr. Watt compared the first sketch
of the weasel prints to the
new, detailed sketch.

Dr. Watt flashed a message.
Hamster Holmes stopped running.
"Yes!" he said. "Things are *not*
always what they seem.
This mystery is . . . solved!"
They went to tell Springy the news.

"In the detailed sketch of the print in the garage," Hamster Holmes explained, "there are lines around the weasel print." Dr. Watt hadn't noticed them when he did the quick sketch!

"What does it mean?"
Springy asked as they walked
to the garage.
"It means that weasels are not
always weasels,"
Hamster Holmes hinted.

And in the garage . . .
there was a young ferret!
"Who are you," Springy asked,
"and where is the weasel?"
The ferret looked scared.
"I'm Alicia," she said quietly,
"and this is all a big mistake."

"This ferret *made* the weasel prints,"
Hamster Holmes said.
Springy was confused.
Alicia showed them her sandals.
"The soles make fake weasel prints,"
she confessed. "I invented them and
stepped in paint to throw you
off my trail. I'm so sorry."

Hamster Holmes said they knew
the prints were fake when they saw
shoe marks around each one.
"They need work," she said.
"It's quite clever," said Springy,
"but if you have great ideas,
why are you stealing mine?"

"I wasn't stealing," Alicia said.
"I was learning."
She had studied his notes,
practiced with his tools,
and even made flippers to help
her swim to the dock entrance
to see his boats.
"I want to be an inventor like you."

"You already are!" he told her.
"I wish you had just asked me. . . .
I love teaching, and I could really
use your help with something!"
Alicia's face lit up.

Springy said, "Ta-da!" and showed
them his secret invention.
"A springy submarine!" Alicia gasped.
Then she asked Springy to
explain how it worked.
Hamster Holmes smiled and said,
"I suspect you two will enjoy
working together as much as
Dr. Watt and I do!"